Try and Try Again

"Let's go skating!" Frank said brightly.

"That's not my kind of fun," said Beth.

"Why don't you have a try?" asked Frank.

Frank sped off as fast as the speed of light. Beth was left behind. She tripped and fell on her thigh.

"I'll sit on the bench. I don't mind.

I'll stay behind," said Beth.

"Let's try again." Frank held her hand.

"Left, right, left, right, left, right!
That's it! You've got it!" said Frank.
Beth grinned with delight.

"Let's go fast! Hold tight!" said Frank. They whizzed by the truck. "Whee! This is wild!" yelled Beth.

"Catch me if you can!" Beth sped off at the speed of light.

"I'm trying!" sighed Frank, from behind.

Questions for discussion:

- Why do you think Beth says that skating is 'not her kind of fun'?

- What does Frank do when Beth falls?

- Why does Frank sigh when he has to catch up with Beth?

Game with /ie/ words

Play as 'Concentration' or use for reading practice. Enlarge and photocopy the page twice on two different colors of card.
Cut the cards up to play.
Ensure the players sound out the words.

Before reading this book, the reader needs to know:

- sounds can be spelled by more than one letter.
- the spellings <igh>, <i> and <y> can represent the sound /ie/.

This book introduces:

- the spellings <igh>, <i> and <y> for the sound /ie/.
- text at 2-syllable level.

Words the reader may need help with:

skating, said, brightly, don't, you, speed, was, her, stay, again, you've, hold, they

Vocabulary:

thigh - the part of the leg between the hip and the knee
grinned - smiled broadly
delight - enjoyment
sigh - to let out one's breath from sadness or tiredness

Talk about the story:

Frank and Beth go skating.
Frank is a good skater, but Beth has a fall.
Will she give up on her first try?

Reading Practice

Practice blending these sounds into words:

igh	i	y
night	hi	my
right	I'm	by
high	child	fly
fight	kind	why
fright	find	try
tight	wild	cry
flight	mind	fry